This book belongs to

Arden

Written by Elanor Best.
Illustrated by Lara Ede.

Taylor Tiptoe

Elanor Best • Lara Ede

make
believe
ideas

Tiny **Taylor** loved to *dance*:
her **feet** would NEVER stop.

She'd **spin** and twist

and

Leap and *twirl,*

then

shimmy,

shake, and **hop**.

For this year's Summer Showcase, **Taylor** longed to get the *chance* to play the leading **princess** and **prove** that she could *dance*.

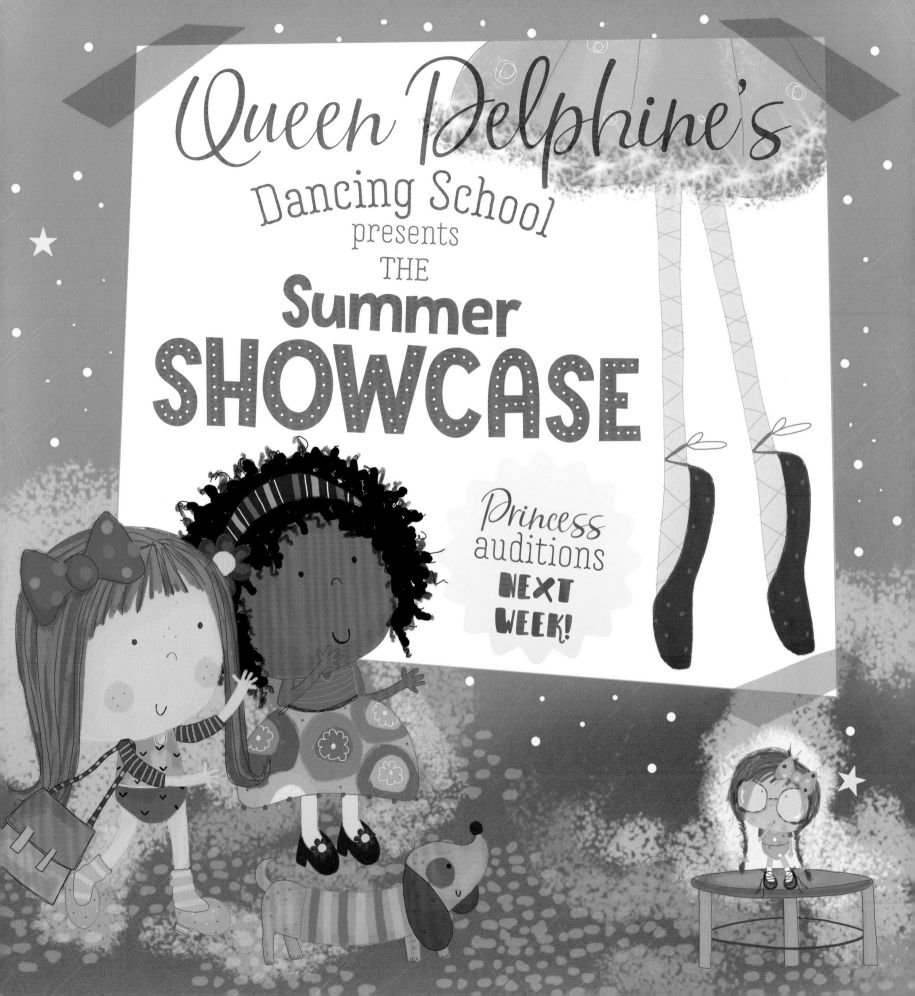

But every time poor **Taylor** tried
to strike a perfect *pose*,
no one seemed to notice
in the sea of *pointed toes*.

In fact, she was so **LITTLE**

and so VERY hard to spot,

the other dancers *passed* right by

this tiny *tutu* dot!

Taylor scratched her head and cried,

"I'm too small to be seen!"

"There's just **one** *dancer* who can **help**:

the magic
Queen Delphine."

So, on her tiptoes **Taylor** skipped along the *winding* street...

and *didn't* stop until she stood at **Delphine's** pointed *feet*.

"My only wish is to be tall," said Taylor, feeling brave.

"I can **help**," the *queen* replied,
and gave her **wand** a *wave*.

Sparkles

fizzled in the air,

around small **Taylor's** toes.

And then she *gasped*

as she **began** . . . .

...to grow

and grow

Now **Taylor** was

GINORMOUS!

She **towered** above the floor,
and **gazed** around at all the things
she *hadn't* seen before.

Queen Delphine's
Dancing School

But back at school, when **Taylor** danced, *everything* went wrong.

BALLET BAG

She couldn't keep her *balance* for her **legs** were far too long.

Worst of all, now she was *tall*, she found she had to duck. She **couldn't** get through **any** door without first getting **stuck!**

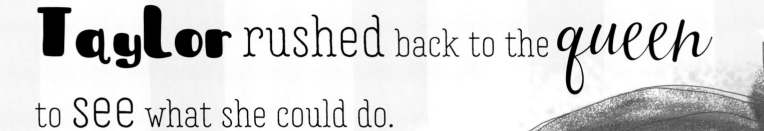

Taylor rushed back to the **queen** to **see** what she could do.

"I've got a **plan**," wise *Delphine* said. "Now **try** just being **YOU!**"

"The secret to good *dancing* is **not** your looks or height.

It's something **within** YOU that shines much **brighter** than the lights!"

Now **Taylor** knew just what to do to get on with her mission.

She took a **breath,** puffed up her chest . . .

and ran to the audition.

With **bravery,** she *leapt* on stage and **pointed** both her feet.

She *whirled* and whizzed and bounced and *fizzed*

and **boogied** to the beat.

The music stopped, and all at once
the judges gave a cheer.

They shouted, "Tiny Taylor
is the princess for this year!"

Summer SHOWCASE

starring
(the tiny but terrific...)

Taylor Tiptoe

For one night only

Queen Delphine's Dancing School Auditorium

Tickets on the door

At last the Summer Showcase came,
and **Taylor** played her part.

She *danced* the best, *despite* her size,

for she danced with all her **heart!**

Taylor's wish had made her learn the **one** thing that was **true**: there's nothing that you **can't** achieve if you *believe* in **YOU!**

Royal box